METHUEN PAIRED READING STORYBOOKS

Bethy Wants A Blue Ice-Cream

Bill Gillham

Illustrated by Margaret Chamberlain

Methuen Children's Books

Bethy went to the sea-side.

She paddled in the sea . . .

until a big wave chased her.

She looked in rock pools . . .

until a crab came
and looked at *her*!

Then she made a sandcastle . . .

but the sea washed it away.

"Never mind," said Mum.
"Let's buy an ice-cream."

Mum had a pink one.

Dad had a chocolate one.

"I want a blue one,"
said Bethy.

"Never heard of blue
ice-cream," said the man.

"Bethy wants a BLUE
ice-cream," said Bethy.

And she started to cry.

"What's the matter?"
asked a policeman.

"She wants a
blue ice-cream," said Dad,
"and there isn't such a thing."

"Why, of course there is!"
said the policeman.

"Give me a pair
of those blue sunglasses –
and a vanilla ice-cream."

He put the sunglasses
on Bethy's nose,

...and the ice-cream in her hand.

The ice-cream *looked* blue
to Bethy . . .

...nd it even *tasted* blue as well!

How to pair read

1 Sit the child next to you, so that you can both see the book.

2 Tell the child you are *both* going to read the story *at the same time.* To begin with the child will be hesitant: adjust your speed so that you are reading almost simultaneously, *pointing to the words* as you go.

3 If the child makes a mistake, repeat the correct word but *keep going* so that fluency is maintained.

4 Gradually increase your speed once you and the child are reading together.

5 As the child becomes more confident, lower your voice and, progressively, try dropping out altogether.

6 If the child stumbles or gets stuck, give the correct word and continue 'pair-reading' to support fluency, dropping out again quite quickly.

7 Read the story *right through* once a day but not more than twice, so that it stays fresh.

8 After about 5–8 readings the child will usually be reading the book independently.

In its original form paired reading was first devised by Roger Morgan and Elizabeth Lyon, and described in a paper published in the Journal of Child Psychology and Psychiatry (1979).

First published in Great Britain in 1986
by Methuen Children's Books Ltd, 11 New Fetter Lane, London EC4P 4EE
Text copyright © 1986 Bill Gillham. Illustrations copyright © 1986 Margaret Chamberlain
Printed in Great Britain ISBN 0 416 95790 0